Railway Series, No. 22

SMALL RAILWAY ENGINES

by
THE REV. W. AWDRY

with illustrations by
PETER AND GUNVOR EDWARDS

KAYE & WARD LIMITED

First published by
Kaye & Ward Ltd 1967
Fifth impression by Kaye & Ward Ltd
The Windmill Press, Kingswood, Tadworth, Surrey
1981

Copyright © 1970 Kaye & Ward Ltd

ISBN 0 7182 0021 7

Printed and bound in Great Britain by
William Clowes (Beccles) Limited, Beccles and London

DEAR FRIENDS,

Some leadmines up in the hills have long been closed, but their waste-heaps still spoil a lovely valley.

The Fat Controller has now found that the waste is good weed-killing railway ballast. He talked to the Owner and the Thin Controller of the Skarloey Railway, and other important people. They "went shares" and built a Small Railway to fetch it away.

The Small Engines are managed by a Controller. They call him the Small Controller; but that is only in fun. He is bigger than either of the others!   THE AUTHOR

The Author gratefully acknowledges the help given by fellow members of the Ravenglass and Eskdale Railway Preservation Society in the preparation of this book.

Ballast

THE Fat Controller's Railway has a new look. From end to end they are clearing old ballast from the track and packing the sleepers with fresh stones. The Gangers are pleased. "Weeds don't grow in it," they say; and even James has stopped grumbling about dirty sidings!

Douglas and Donald disappeared regularly behind the Big Station, along a line on which none of the others had ever gone. They returned with loaded ballast trains, and were most mysterious about it.

"Verra wee engines bring the ballast doun fra the hills" was all they would say.

Soon the engines could talk of nothing else. James and Henry thought the "Verra wee engines" must be some kind of magic.

"I don't believe it," said Gordon. "Donald and Douglas have pulled our wheels before."

But Duck wanted to see for himself, so he asked permission to take some trucks. When he arrived, he was told to push them under the "chute". This was like a tunnel made of steel girders. On top of it stood some queer-looking trucks.

"What d'you think of our 'chute'?" said a voice. "Good, isn't it?"

Duck blinked. Standing beside him was a small green engine.

"Where did you spring from?" asked Duck.

"I've been here all the time," smiled the small engine. "I'm Rex, and you, I'm sure, are Duck."

"How *did* you know?"

"That's easy; there's only one Great Western engine in these parts."

There was a sudden rattling and roaring. Duck's whole train shuddered.

"Wh-what was that?" he asked, startled.

"That was our 'chute'. The bottoms of those wagons slide out, and the stones fall through the chute into your trucks. We may be small, but we're quite efficient."

Duck puffed away much impressed.

Next time, there were three Small Engines. Rex introduced Duck to Bert and Mike. "As you can see," he went on, "the Small Controller's given us different coats."

"Silly nonsense," grumbled Mike.

"I *like* being blue," protested Bert.

"It's all right for *you*," fumed Mike, "but not for me. Passengers'll say I look like a pillar-box!"

"Shocking!" said Rex, and winked at Duck. "Consider *my* feelings. When we were both green, passengers kept calling me Mike!"

"You . . . you . . ." spluttered Mike.

"Stow it you two," said Bert. "Duck," he went on, "have you seen our coaches?"

"Where are they?" asked Duck.

"Over there," said Bert.

"But they're tru . . . I mean they're not like ours," he finished lamely.

Rex smiled. "I agree. They are like trucks, but they behave surprisingly well."

"Sez you," put in Mike rudely.

"They're all right," said Bert, "if you treat 'em right. Besides, passengers like 'em. They won't use 'covereds' on a fine day. It's this scenery — you know, trees, mountains and such — can't understand it myself; but then, passengers are queer."

"You're right there," said Mike. "Give me goods trains every time."

"Do you *like* trucks?" Duck was surprised.

"Not all of them," smiled Mike, "but our big ballast hoppers are different. They run on bogies as sweetly as any coach. We take them to the old mines, fill them up, and run them down here to the chute. The men pull some levers, and the whole lot's unloaded before you can say 'Small Controller'. No trouble at all."

"How about hot axleboxes?" put in Rex.

"We soon cured *that* nonsense."

"You mean the Small Controller did!"

"Same thing," grinned Mike.

Duck chuckled delightedly. Rex and Mike loved teasing each other.

"I can't understand," said Duck, "why I've never heard about you before."

The Small engines all answered at once.

"We've only just come . . ."

". . . from our Railway in England which closed."

". . . Your Fat Controller asked us to come and fetch ballast for him . . ."

". . . and he said he'd bring us plenty of passengers too."

"Haven't you had passengers before?" asked Duck.

"Only in England. It's our first season here."

"Oh!" promised Duck. "Then I'll bring you lots. Goodbye! Goodbye!" and he puffed excitedly away to see about it.

Tit for Tat

THE engines were being cleaned and polished for the day. Bert, who was going out first, had a tall chimney in his funnel to draw up his fire.

"We've got Visitors today," said his Driver.

Rex yawned. "We have 'em every day," grunted Mike.

"But these are Special," said the Driver. "One takes 'moving pictures', and the other writes books. So mind you all behave."

"I don't want to be a moving picture in a book," protested Bert. "I want to stay as I am."

They all tried to explain, but Bert was still muddled when he went to take his train.

The visitors were clergymen, one fat, the other thin. They arrived in a little car. Both had cameras.

They shook hands with Bert's Driver. "The Small Controller," he told them, "says you can ride with me in Bert's tender, if you like."

"Thank you," they said. "May we come later please? Just now, the sun is shining so nicely that we want to take photographs."

Then they asked Bert his name and told him how smart he looked.

"These visitors," he thought, "do at least know how to speak to engines."

He puffed away feeling happier.

Wherever the line came near the road – Level crossings, Bridges, Stations – there the two clergymen were, squinting into their cameras.

Bert found this rather upsetting. "They might wave at an engine," he complained.

"They can't wave *and* get good pictures," said his Driver; but Bert didn't understand. He thought they were being unfriendly.

"Poop! Poop!" The little car shot past them once more, but Bert made no reply.

"They'll be at the Lane next."

The Lane is a side-road. It runs for a short distance alongside the railway. There is no fence.

It had rained hard in the night. There were puddles in the Lane. The Thin Clergyman sat in the car. The Fat One waited with his camera. He took his pictures, jumped in, and off they went, racing the train to the lane's end.

Unluckily, just as they passed Bert, they went through a puddle.

"Schloooooosh" – muddy water splashed over Bert's boiler.

"Ouch!" said Bert.

But the clergymen didn't know. They were ahead and out of the car. Smiling they waited for Bert to catch up.

Bert wasn't smiling. "They did it on purpose," he snorted crossly.

"They splashed me! They SPLASHED me!" Bert hissed, rolling into the last station.

"Pictures indeed!" he grumbled, running round his train.

"I'm a nice picture; covered in mud!"

He sizzled crossly when the Fat Clergyman sat in his tender for the journey back. "Driver oughtn't to allow him after what he's done!"

Suddenly he stopped sizzling, and let off steam "Whoooooooooosh!"

"I know," he thought, "how to pay the Fat One out. It's a *lovely* plan. I only wish the Thin One was there too," he said. But he said it to himself.

Bert ran nicely till they reached the Woods.

The line climbs steeply here. Bert usually "rushes" the hill. This time, he deliberately dawdled.

"Come on!" said his Driver giving him full steam.

This was just what Bert wanted.

"Tit for Tat! TIT for TAT!" he shouted, storming up the slope.

Rain-soaked branches met close overhead. Bert's blast, shooting straight up, shook them wildly. Showers of water fell on Clergyman and Driver. Their soaking did not stop till they had topped the rise, and steam could be reduced for the downward run.

The Small Controller soon found out what had happened. He sent Bert back to the Shed. "You're a Very Naughty Engine," he said sternly. "I won't have rudeness to visitors."

"They *splashed* me," faltered Bert. "I only..."

"That's no excuse. I'm ashamed of you."

Bert went sadly away.

But he was happy again when Rex and Mike came in.

"Those Visitors are Nice," he told them. "They came and said 'sorry', and I said 'sorry' too. Then they cleaned me like Driver does. They know lots about Engines," he went on. "The Thin One's writing about me in a book. He promised he'd write about you too. Think of that!"

Mike's Whistle

ONE morning when he arrived, Duck's whistle was out of order. They had worked late the night before and his Driver and Fireman had used it to boil eggs for their supper.

But something had gone wrong, and next morning, when he wanted to whistle, Duck found he could only make burpling noises. He was upset about it.

"Never mind," said his Driver, "it must be a bit of that egg which broke. We'll clean it out presently when we've got time. Meanwhile, no one will mind."

But Mike made rude remarks about it.

"Shplee! Shplee!" mimicked Mike. "It's shocking! If engines can't whistle properly, they shouldn't try."

"Then why do you?" asked Bert.

"Why do I what?"

"Try to whistle, of course."

"Shut up! You're jealous." Mike was proud of his shrill whistle. "Mine's better than yours, anyway."

"Listen, Mike," said Rex. "If I had a whistle like yours, d'you know what I'd do?" He paused impressively. "I'd lose it."

"The idea!" spluttered Mike. "Whistles are important, let me tell you. Engines without whistles aren't proper engines at all."

Mike went redder than ever with fury. His steam pressure went up suddenly, and his safety-valves blew off, "Whooooooosh!"

"Hullo!" said his Driver. "As you're ready first, you'd better take the 'passenger'."

"What! and leave my 'goods'?"

"Yes, Bert can do that. We can't have you blowing off in here. Come on!"

Mike backed down on the coaches "whooooo-shing" angrily. When all was ready, he started with a rude jerk. "Come on! Come on! COME ON!" he puffed.

"What's bitten him?" wondered his Driver. "He doesn't like coaches, but he's never been as bad as this."

Mike whistled loudly at the least excuse. "They're jealous, they're jealous," he muttered as he bucketted along. "I'll show 'em! I'll show 'em!"

"He's in a flaming temper about something," remarked his Driver. He was relieved when they reached the End Station safely. He looked Mike all over, but saw nothing wrong. He tried to soothe him, but Mike still sizzled crossly. "It beats me," he said at last.

Then, soon after they had started back, he heard a thin persistent tinkle. "That's something loose on his boiler," he thought. "I'll tighten it at the next Station."

But he never got the chance.

It was the cow's fault. She stood on the track busily cropping grass. She took no notice of the train.

Mike stopped. He wasn't frightened. He had met her before. She only made him cross.

He came slowly forward whooshing steam from his cylinders. "Shooooh! Shooooh! Shooooh!"

The cow just flicked her tail and went on eating. Mike felt exasperated.

He tried whistling. He wanted to say "Get out of my way you stupid animal!" but he didn't get far. His second "peep" turned into a tremendous "Whoooooosh!" as his whistle-cap shot up like a rocket, and landed in a field.

Driver and Guard started to look for it, but some passengers objected. "We can't waste time with whistles," they said. "We must catch our train."

Mike was dismayed. "There are boards saying 'WHISTLE'," he protested. "I mustn't pass those without whistling. That's 'Orders'. Please find it."

"Sorry," said the passengers. "We can't wait. We'll have to whistle for you; that's all." And so it was arranged.

Whenever they saw a board, Guard, Driver, and passengers all whistled. They made more noise than Mike ever did, and thought it splendid fun.

Mike mourned for his lost whistle.

Mike hoped his Driver would give him a new whistle when they got home. He was disappointed.

"I've no spare whistles," said the Small Controller sternly. "So you'll have to wait. It serves you right for being such a crosspatch."

Mike worked in the quarries for the rest of the day. It was nearly dark when he reached the Shed.

"What's that?" asked Bert, as Mike came in.

"Shsh!" whispered Rex. "Take no notice. It's an Improper Engine."

"Why Improper? He looks all right to me."

"It's got no whistle."

"Oh dear!" said Bert. "How shocking! We don't approve of his sort, do we?"

Useful Railway

MIKE had had trouble with some sheep. He grumbled about them dreadfully.

"They're silly," said Rex, "but they're useful."

"What!"

"Farmers," went on Rex, "sell their wool."

"What's that?"

"People make clothes from wool. You know – things they wear instead of paint."

"Quite right, Rex." The engines were startled. The Small Controller stood in the doorway. "The farmers," he went on, "want us to take their wool to market. If we do it well, they'll know we're Really Useful. So you must all do your best."

"But I don't understand, Sir," Bert protested. "We can't drive sheep down the line. They wouldn't go straight."

"Silly!" said Rex. "We don't drive sheep, we take their wool, in bales on trucks. It'll be easy."

The Small Controller laughed. "Very well, Rex," he said. "You seem to know all about it, so you shall take the first train."

They started loading at the Lane. Then Rex came gently down the line stopping at all the farms and level crossings on the way.

"Nearly finished," said his Driver at last. "Only one more load, and we're away."

But he'd reckoned without Willie.

Willie was late. He'd been dawdling. Rex's whistle roused him, and he set off at top speed.

"Your load's slipping," someone shouted.

"Oh dear!" thought Willie. "I can't stop now. I hope it'll hold."

It did, but not quite long enough. Willie dashed into the Yard, and swept round to bring his trailer alongside the line. The trailer tilted, the strain loosened the ropes, and the topmost wool-bales slid sideways to the track.

"Crumbs!" burst out Willie. "That's torn it! I must warn Rex."

He jumped down and ran along the line.

Rex's trucks were running nicely. "I *said* it was easy! I *said* it was easy!" he chuntered happily to himself.

Then everything happened at once. Willie waved and shouted, and behind Willie, through the bridge, Rex glimpsed the bales lying on the track.

"Stop! Stop! STOP!" he whistled.

"On! On! ON!" urged the stupid trucks.

But Rex's brakes checked them. "Oooooer!" he groaned, and shut his eyes. His front hit something soft. He tilted sideways, and found himself off the line leaning against the Cutting side, while his Driver felt him all over to find if he was hurt.

When the Small Controller came, Willie said he was very sorry, and, with his master's permission, he stayed and worked very hard clearing the mess.

They put the trucks to rights, and Bert lost no time in taking them away.

But Rex had to stay where he was. He didn't like that a bit.

Trains kept passing, and passengers would point at him and say "Oooh! Look! There's been an accident!"

Mike and Bert would laugh and remark how easy it was to pull wool trains.

Poor Rex.

They lifted Rex to the rails at last and Bert and Mike helped him home.

"That accident served me right for being swanky."

"No," said Bert. "It wasn't your fault at all."

"Sorry we laughed." This came from Mike.

The Small Controller was waiting. "I'm proud of you all," he said. "Thanks to Rex, the accident did little harm. Bert and Mike worked like heroes, and our customers all admire the way we managed. They thought we were a 'toy railway', but now they say we're Really Useful. They've promised us plenty more work when the wool traffic is done."

If you have enjoyed these stories, you will also enjoy a visit to the Ravenglass and Eskdale Railway in Cumberland.